Mini Sagas

YORKSHIRE & LINCOLNSHIRE

First published in Great Britain in 2010 by
Young Writers, Remus House, Coltsfoot Drive,
Peterborough, PE2 9JX
Tel (01733) 890066 Fax (01733) 313524
Website: www.youngwriters.co.uk

Disclaimer
Young Writers has maintained every effort
to publish stories that will not cause offence.
Any stories, events or activities relating to individuals
should be read as fictional pieces and not construed
as real-life character portrayal.

Design by Spencer Hart

Foreword

Since Young Writers was established in 1990, our aim has been to promote and encourage written creativity amongst children and young adults. By giving aspiring young authors the chance to be published, Young Writers effectively nurtures the creative talents of the next generation, allowing their confidence and writing ability to grow.

With our latest fun competition, *The Adventure Starts Here …* , secondary school children nationwide were given the tricky challenge of writing a story with a beginning, middle and an end in just fifty words.

The diverse and imaginative range of entries made the selection process a difficult but enjoyable task with stories chosen on the basis of style, expression, flair and technical skill. A fascinating glimpse into the imaginations of the future, we hope you will agree that this entertaining collection is one that will amuse and inspire the whole family.

Contents

Queen Elizabeth's Grammar School, Alford

Queen Elizabeth's High School, Gainsborough

The Grammar School at Leeds, Leeds

Whitcliffe Mount School, Cleckheaton

Emma Russell 227
Matthew Deighton (13) 228
Sophie Edwards 229
Jake Johnson (14) 230
Amy McAllister 231
Raad Gorji 232
Holly Beech-Clough 233
Thomas McVey 234
Stephanie Kiss 235
Tayler Wells 236
Matthew Clough (13) 237
Danny Barker 238
Luke Johnson (14) 239
Lewis Goodyer (14) 240
William Hardy 241
Conner Luke Phillips 242
John Britton (14) 243
Xavia Timothy 244
Georgia Grogan 245
Amie Garfield (13) 246
Paige Ives 247
Ashley Davies 248
Lauren Clark (13) 249
William Deakin 250
Ross Anthony Clough 251
James Hendry 252
Ben McDonald (14) 253
Cameron Bell (14) 254
Georgie Holmes 255
Alex Clayton (13) 256
Bradley Kirk 257
Saul Sceats (14) 258
Leah Smith 259
Thomas Richardson 260
Jake Lambert (13) 261
Jake Inman 262
Robert Davey (13) 263
Cameron Robson (14) 264
Michael Craig (13) 265
Oliver Hunt 266
Emma Rhodes 267
Emma Stirk 268
Louise Reynolds 269
Jade Louise Mair 270
Nathan Oakey 271
Bradley Marsden 272
Joe Bradley 273
Jack Daniels 274

The Mini Sagas

Cats

I'm alone in the graveyard at night. All I see is the
moonlight shimmering on the headstones. On top
of a large one is a big black cat, with bright green
eyes, staring at me. My body starts to shake all
over. I have a phobia of big black cats.

Tiffany Partington (16)
Catcote School, Hartlepool

The Lost Swimming Pool

A little boy walked to a swimming pool to see his dad. He got lost and he asked an old man, 'Where is the swimming pool? My dad works there. Can you help me?'
The old man pointed.
'Oh, yes! I can see it. I wasn't looking properly. Thank you!'

Sean Wray (13)
Catcote School, Hartlepool

2

Bonfire Night

On Bonfire Night there was a man near the fire.
His trousers were on fire. The fire spread up his
legs onto his body, his arms, his head and his face
and he was burnt. Then I noticed he was the guy,
Guy Fawkes. Then we had a party.

David Scott (11)

Catcote School, Hartlepool

3

The Broken Earring

Me and my older sisters were going to the park
for a long walk, but I broke my earring, so I have
to go to the earring shop to have it repaired.
When I got there, they were all stolen and I could
not replace my beautiful, dangly, golden earring.

Chelsea Bennett (12)

Catcote School, Hartlepool

My Pet Dog

My pet dog went to the vets and got checked out.
He was OK. He is a different kind of dog.
I went home in a flash. I got a dog bowl out and
filled it with bones. My pet dog is called Rebel and
he is a golden retriever.

George Coxon (11)
Catcote School, Hartlepool

The Lost Tomb

One night, there was a tomb in Egypt. It was dark and cold and one of the tombs was full of gold. As we walked down the passageway, we could hear sounds coming from a tomb. It was scary. As we waited in the door, Tutankhamun had a mask.

James Elener (13)
Catcote School, Hartlepool

Tara And Jackson

I take them for a walk, play with them. I
sometimes give them biscuits and try and make
them happy. I am going to take them to my
mam's house and then to the beach. I stroke
them a lot. What are they? They are my dogs,
Tara and Jackson.

Caitlin Martin (12)
Catcote School, Hartlepool

7

Untitled

I met a friend. Her name was Amy. We went on
lots of rides at Bush Gardens and ate lots and lots
of ice cream. We went to 'Wet and Wild' and had
lots of fun, but then I realised that Amy wasn't
real. I didn't know who she was!

Lauren Briggs (13)

Catcote School, Hartlepool

Poppy The Dog

We got the dog. We called her Poppy.
In the next 14 years she caused so much havoc, it
was unbelievable. She ate the sofa, ran away tied
to a table, with the table, got wrapped around
lamp posts. We didn't realise how much we loved
her, until she died.

James Buckton (13)
Hornsea School & Language College, Hornsea

9

The Boys We Love, The Lessons We Learn

Zoe tells Sarah she loved Tom, but Sarah loves him too. Tom gets with Zoe. Sarah has an argument with Zoe. Zoe is nasty about Tom. He finds out and finishes with her. He gets with Sarah. Then Sarah and Zoe become friends again and Zoe finds a new boyfriend.

Jessica Close (13)

Hornsea School & Language College, Hornsea

Tilly The Clumsy Witch

Loved up. That's how Tilly the clumsy witch felt
when she saw Max, the wizard. But when she
saw him, she would embarrass herself and today
was no exception. She tumbled and rolled all
over Grumpy Gnome's pansies. Max looked and
smiled. 'I still love you, though you *are* clumsy!'

Holly Brown (14)

Hornsea School & Language College, Hornsea

11

Does Love Last?

Fourteen-year-old best friends, Molly and Lucy,
meet up with some older boys. They had a laugh,
then went home. Danny asked Molly out. Molly
said yes, but Joe likes Molly.
After two months they break up. Molly and Joe
get close. Will they get together? Will Danny care?

Philippa Walker (13)

Hornsea School & Language College, Hornsea

Grandma's Secret Life

Lucy Cooper is staying at her grandma's house whilst her parents are on holiday. She and her brother, George, are not looking forward to staying over, but they arrive to find out that their sweet, old grandma is actually an international superstar in disguise. Will they keep Grandma's secret?

Alice Drewery (13)

Hornsea School & Language College, Hornsea

Deal With The Devil

An old man named Graham dies in his local pub.
He makes a deal with the Devil to live forever.
After ten years, Graham wants to die, so he
challenges the Devil to a game of darts. It is a
draw, so they have a deciding game of American
pool.

Joe Scarfe (13)
Hornsea School & Language College, Hornsea

The Well

I was curious about the well. It was covered with
weeds, cobwebs and all things imaginable. I had
wondered all day if it held water. I looked in. I
couldn't see, but I soon found out that there was
water …

Wesley Andrews (14)

Hornsea School & Language College, Hornsea

The Final Straw

He could feel his heart beating heavily underneath his school shirt. Shaking, he took the knife off the kitchen counter. He fingered it curiously for a moment, then ran the cold blade along his skin. Then, in one quick movement, he plunged it into his flesh. His pain was over …

Lauren Ireland (13)

Hornsea School & Language College, Hornsea

The Shadow Of Mystery

I got into the cab. The mysterious figure in the driver's seat didn't look quite right. It turned around. Its sharp teeth bared. Its dark eyes beaming. I felt a tearing of my skin - I was fleshless and lifeless.

Ruby Butler (13)
Hornsea School & Language College, Hornsea

Unconventional

Although I had only been in here for a couple of hours, I couldn't help but wonder about my baby, Jack. He had just started to walk yesterday. Whilst I was daydreaming, a loud, deep voice and two barking dogs broke me out of my trance. 'Where is he?'

Ryan Daubney (13)
Hornsea School & Language College, Hornsea

Cornered

Lieutenant Leyland, cornered in a forest by Nazis, laying traps, shooting and running, he finds a place to hide. He hears them speak in German. Then a group shriek, as the other Germans run towards the scream, Leyland jumps out and fires. As they fall down, he cheers.

Benjamin Rothery (12)

Hornsea School & Language College, Hornsea

19

Lost

I ran along the winding street. I was lost, I was scared, I was worried. It was getting dark. All of a sudden, alcoholics surrounded me. What to do? Then *bang,* my nose, my eyes, my face, covered in blood. 'Help me!' I shouted. Or would it be too late?

Luci Clarke (11)

Hornsea School & Language College, Hornsea

Shadows

It was coming after her, something, someone, pounding after her. *Thud! Thud!* She turned around, terrified to face it. She froze. Icy shivers trickled down her spine. The smell of scarlet blood filled the air. It was a spirit coming to suck out her soul. Before she knew it … *dead!*

Samantha Osborne (11)

Hornsea School & Language College, Hornsea

Mum's Mysterious Meeting

Tim trembled as he listened through the door.
What was his mum playing at?
'I'll take that one please,' she said.
'Ah, yes, killed that one with my own fair hand,'
said a voice.
Suddenly, his mum came out the door. 'Tim,
honey, do you like my new sheepskin coat?'

Daisy Stericker (11)
Hornsea School & Language College, Hornsea

22

The Outback

The Australian outback is as plain as plain. There is nothing for miles, but there, I saw water! I ran and ran, but it's an illusion. I sat down and waited a few moments. I saw a Jeep. It was a safari tour. I was saved! Let's go to freedom!

Gianni Raise (11)

Hornsea School & Language College, Hornsea

23

The Angry Fish

'Ugh!' moaned the fish, 'Why am I never allowed to do anything, not even go to school! Apparently, I'm not brave enough. I go swimming on my own!'
'You can't go to school, as you are too young,' Nemo's dad.
'Yeah, but I'm not too young! Oh, my goodness!'

Abbie Cockill (13)
Hornsea School & Language College, Hornsea

The Special Cauldron

The pot bubbled slowly and stickily, as the substance got hotter and hotter. The cauldron melted with the heat and the hot, sticky substance spread all over the floor. 'Oh, no! That cauldron was special!'
'What's going on here?' the terrible voice of the factory owner bellowed.
They cowered.

Rebecca Wood (12)

Hornsea School & Language College, Hornsea

25

Not Quite Heaven

The dyke was never dry, but today it was dry. I
walked along it until I came to a stop - there was
a door, just laid in the mud. It opened to reveal
Heaven. Suddenly, I fell down. I was trapped.
Why was I in Heaven? When did I die?

Kate Dean

Hornsea School & Language College, Hornsea

Pressure On Chelsea In Champions League

Chelsea take the kick-off and pass it around the field, player to player. Then Barcelona get a penalty in the 85th minute. They miss it. Chelsea kick it up field and score a fantastic goal. Then the whistle blows. Chelsea win the Champions League. Chelsea lift the cup.

Greg Cousins (11)

Hornsea School & Language College, Hornsea

Perfect Dreams

He snuck up behind her, failing to resist her luxurious blood. He shuddered at the memory of hurting her. She looked back, catching a glimpse of the pale, yet gorgeous, vampire … she woke to find herself back in the forest. Staring at her, he said, 'Dreaming about me again?'

Hannah Lawson

Hornsea School & Language College, Hornsea

Fast And Furious

Vin Diesel was walking to his beast of a car, so were the other contestants. As soon as he got in his car, he gave the other drivers dirty looks, then the cars went zooming off. You could see the flames from the tyres and the exhausts. Vin Diesel won!

Rosie Cunningham (11)

Hornsea School & Language College, Hornsea

29

Taken Over

Rain came down. The smell of old rotten meat and odours stained the battlefield. The castle wasn't ready. When the stones came down like shooting stars, it went black. As the castle fell, the creatures went first. That was it. The fortress had been taken by horrible, ugly creatures.

Ian Simpson (11)

Hornsea School & Language College, Hornsea

Fast And Furious

Bryan wanders into the closed garage. The
engine's roaring, ready to race. On the track,
people cheering, glamorous cars posing.
Bryan, Mark and Angela wander to the turbo-
charged cars. Bryan, in his flash blue car, edges
into the lead. Round the death corner, Bryan leads
… wins! Cops turn up!

Steven Clarke (12)

Hornsea School & Language College, Hornsea

Life-Changing Decision

Thousands of people were auditioning. Only six could come out on top. After stressing and arguing, six were decided.

Weeks went past, dancing and singing. Only two were left! Who was it going to be, Luci or Josh? Long hours of practising came down to this moment. Judges announce - *'Luci - winner!'*

Bethany Haworth (12)
Hornsea School & Language College, Hornsea

32

Waiting!

Tick-tock, tick-tock, foot tapping, hair twiddling
and pen jiggling, *blah … blah … blah …* boring!
It's my turn to answer. *'Erm? 62?'* The tension in
my head is burning like a roaring fire. Did I get it
right? Finally, just in time, the bell rings.
'Are ya coming, Bess?'

Holly Clarke
Hornsea School & Language College, Hornsea

My Diet Of Starvation

I crept down the stairs, *creak!* The last step, I was there. It looked so great. I ran forward, ripped the fridge door open. I began shoving food in my mouth. I felt amazing, fabulous. Then it hit me. What I was doing. I realised how it was so wrong.

Shauna Herfield Barriskell

Hornsea School & Language College, Hornsea

The First Descent

Zoom! As the kayak flew down grade six rapids.
It's the first descent, so he doesn't know what's
round the next corner. *'Waza?'* As he flies right
into the middle of a hole, which sucks him down
and holds him and holds him until suddenly, it
spits him out!

Luke Cooper

Hornsea School & Language College, Hornsea

Jaws

Snap! Snap! Went the jaws of the shark, as it swerved all over, trying to snatch a fish. It seemed like a battle between life and death, but then it stopped. The shark could no longer see the fish. It had disappeared into the deep blue, unkind, big, murky ocean.

Zak Chambers

Hornsea School & Language College, Hornsea

Will She Find Out?

'Ow!' screamed Lucie, as she leapt out of the seat.
'Next!' shouted the piercing man.
'Argh!' yelled Lizzie.
Lucie and Lizzie walked out of the piercing shop
and walked back home. They sneaked into the
house and ran upstairs. She was there. They
turned around. She looked. *'Oops!* Busted!'

Georgia Fortnum (11)
Hornsea School & Language College, Hornsea

37

Christmas Eve Ghost

There is a girl, old and broken and crooked.
She will never die. She will never leave. She is
the ghost of Christmas Eve. She must be over a
hundred now. She will take your present when
on the prowl. So watch out and look for her - a
small, little girl.

Nikita Griffiths (11)
Hornsea School & Language College, Hornsea

Horrid Henry And The Large Smash

Horrid Henry was pestering his little brother, Peter. *Smash! Shriek!* 'Sounds like Mum!' said Peter with a gasp. The boys went down to investigate. It turned out Peter Andre was coming to town. Mum dropped her cup of tea. It smashed.

Katy White
Hornsea School & Language College, Hornsea

39

Untitled

Panting in fear, as the man with the human skin mask slowly walked up, smashing every box in his way, getting closer. Suddenly, the noise stopped. Everything went silent. He glanced over the box. He's gone. He wipes the tears from his eyes and slowly gets up and runs away.

Roan Stanley (13)
Hornsea School & Language College, Hornsea

Snatched

It was Christmas Eve. All was quiet. I was sitting in front of the TV, snuggled up with a blanket, when all of a sudden, this hand grabbed me from behind and put me into a sack of presents! Olivia sent me a text … 'Sorry, I wanted a friend for Christmas!'

Cara Webster

Hornsea School & Language College, Hornsea

41

The Shadow

Lucas sees a shadow from his room, gets up, goes to investigate. He slowly opens the door, creeps into the garden. There's the shadow, on the tree - he steps slowly - he smells a foul odour, of rotting fish guts. He slips on a wet bone, falls to the floor, dead.

Jason Swann (12)

Hornsea School & Language College, Hornsea

Birth Beginning

Tom was fascinated by cloning. The fact that
humanity could act as God, creating life …
On the last day of humanity's existence,
Tom went for a visit to the National Genetic
Engineering base. Tom was about to discover
that he would be the cause of the annihilation of
humanity …

Freddie Causton (13)

Hornsea School & Language College, Hornsea

43

Scary Movie

This film was scary. It was called 'House of Wax'.
Bang! The house exploded! *Boom!* It continued for
five minutes. Then a scream. Everybody jumped
out of their seats. The film continued. The music
got louder. Then a girl's head was chopped off!

Reece Etherington (13)
Hornsea School & Language College, Hornsea

Brother Bear

There is a bear who lives with people. His
brother makes fun of him, because he is a bear,
so he packed his bag and lived on the streets. His
parents called the police and they went looking
for him. They found him in a river - dead!

Hollie Fisher (14)

Hornsea School & Language College, Hornsea

45

Football Match!

Goal! Gerrard scores! The stadium went riot
at Anfield. Gerrard passed to Babel, he shot.
Suddenly a big bang - it hit the post. Then Torres
collected the ball and scored.
In the second half, Chelsea got the ball, then
Drogba shot - and missed!
'Ah!' they shouted, 'That was rubbish, Drogba!'

Luke Huby (13)
Hornsea School & Language College, Hornsea

Dead Centipede

Jeff centipede leapt on the stage and walked over to the spotlight. As soon as he was visible, the audience burst into applause. Then there was a flash - blood squirted out of Jeff and he fell to the floor. He had been shot. He was dead and covered in blood.

James Hotchkin (12)

Hornsea School & Language College, Hornsea

My Fight!

Walking home, she was behind me. Her friends chased and caught me. She came up and pushed me. I pushed her back. That's when it all started. Everyone was cheering for her. We carried on for five minutes. In the end, I won, because I punched her in the nose.

Evie Dixon (13)

Hornsea School & Language College, Hornsea

The Street Race

Vroom! The car engine roars, getting ready for the street race. 'Go!' shouted the starting man. *Screech!* As the cars go *zoom!* Police follow the people in the cars speeding off in fear. When suddenly, *bang!* One of the cars tips over and explodes, flames roaring everywhere!

Davis Groves (12)

Hornsea School & Language College, Hornsea

The Boy Saw No Fear

One crisp, warm, autumn evening, David walked in from school, only to find a strange-looking man in the kitchen. The man signalled to someone and four men came in, marching dramatically. David stormed upstairs and found Sweeney Todd butchering a little man, but David never saw any fear.

Ben James Bailey (12)
Hornsea School & Language College, Hornsea

Nasty Prank

Ben sat in the living room, trying to figure out where the banging came from. He couldn't figure it out. It was all over the house, same volume in each room! Suddenly, there were stomping sounds going downstairs. It wasn't anyone going downstairs, it came from the radio!

Kieran Carr (12)

Hornsea School & Language College, Hornsea

Man Utd Vs Chelsea - Cup Premier League

Kick-off. Man Utd start with the ball. Drogba
gets the ball, runs down, but Vidic gets it, passes.
Rooney runs down, shoots, misses! Whistle
blows. Penalties! Berbatov shoots … *goal,* top
corner. Drogba, crossbar - Rooney … *goal!* Cole
… *goal!* Two more people, Valencia, *save!* Terry
misses. Man Utd win!

Tom Coates (12)

Hornsea School & Language College, Hornsea

Horrid Henry

Dark night, trees swaying, cold sweeping towards the house. 'Ow!' yelled Peter. Mum came from downstairs and barged through the door. A shock came to Mum's face. 'Get off him now, Henry!' Mum yelled. Henry stood up in a flash. Mum was talking to him. The last word was - 'Bed!'

Beth Vickers

Hornsea School & Language College, Hornsea

Death To All

The two armies stared, waiting for the charge
by their opponent. One of the knights charged,
followed by the rest. Shields shattered, swords
snapped, men died! One of the ones who was in
charge of the knights fell and an opposing knight
cut his head clean off. He died. Victory!

Oliver Gregory (12)
Hornsea School & Language College, Hornsea

The Drag Race

They started at the lights, their engines revving.
The lights went green. They shot off, wheels
smoking. Who was going to win? They were
halfway through, but they started slowing down.
Then the blue car was spinning all over. Was he
going to crash? No! He saved it!

Jonas Wright
Hornsea School & Language College, Hornsea

Dragged Into The Hellish Abyss

The fires of Hell were screaming beneath her, the ground torn apart by vicious tremors. Then came the demons. Grasping at any part of her, they gradually began to drag her into the Hellish abyss, slowly and painfully incinerating her in the process. Her tortured screams echoed for all eternity.

Grant Zeebroek (15)
King Edward VI Grammar School, Louth

The Diving Competition

My heart pounded, pumping the blood, filled with writhing adrenaline. A muffled cheer sounded as I stepped to the end of the polished board. Hands held high. Eyes closed. I flew: twirling, whirling, spinning, winning. Straight as a poker, I glided into the water. Another cheer erupted: a perfect score.

Alice Blackwell (12)

King Edward VI Grammar School, Louth

Ready Or Not

Kate took a step into the cold, dark room. A shadow moved across the small sliver of light showing through the dusty window from a street light outside. Kate ducked behind an old chest of drawers.

'Ready or not, here I come!' came the little voice of Billy Black.

Kirsty Wivell (13)

King Edward VI Grammar School, Louth

The Way My Friend And I Died

It's been exactly a year since Lucy was killed. I was her best friend. 'Olivia, could you help me please?' the janitor asked.
'Yeah, sure.'
I followed him into the storage room. The door snapped shut. Something flashed in the janitor's hand.
'You need to follow your friend to death!'

Isabelle Leggett (13)
King Edward VI Grammar School, Louth

The Bomb

Is it red or blue? Damn! There's a green! *Ah!* Come on, think, think! Red, blue or green? Let's do green. *Click!* Oh, thank goodness! *Argh!* It's going faster! Oh, no! Red or blue? *Red or blue? Boom!* Program terminated.

Jonathan Dexter (13)
King Edward VI Grammar School, Louth

The Scary Green Eyes

Jack walked into the house. He was confused. Why were there no lights on? Where was his mum? She told him this morning she would be home. Then suddenly, there came a creak from the landing upstairs. He steadily walked up the stairs, scared. Small, green eyes appeared from nowhere!

Heather Ball (13)

King Edward VI Grammar School, Louth

The Boat

'What a night!' said Robert. We admired the stars, with the soft swishing of the sea at our ears. Perfect. But the waves hastened. The tide gained strength. The boat got weak. We sprung a leak and before we knew it, we were going down. We both struggled to breathe …

Bianca Sylvester (13)
King Edward VI Grammar School, Louth

The New Girl

I walk in. All eyes are on me. Like lasers scorching
my skin. I take a seat. Everyone is waiting for me
to make a sound, to move. Someone the other
side of the classroom, is whispering. I have to
speak. 'Class, let's start the lesson.'

Jessica Sanderson (13)
King Edward VI Grammar School, Louth

2010

He walked down the street, *bang!* The sun was approaching Earth, getting faster and faster, closer and closer. The heat was unbearable. So hot. People shouting, animals howling and then … silence. Was this the end … ?

Freddie Moiser (13)
King Edward VI Grammar School, Louth

Time

My head feels light. I'm in space, bobbing around nothingness. I can see for miles - amazing! I turn around. A doctor? He starts shaking me and calling my name. *Ow!* My eyes - a bright light blinding me. People crowding over me, staring; I had woken! Finally, after 30 years!

Camilla Findlay (13)
King Edward VI Grammar School, Louth

It Is Not Possible

It was hell trying to write a story in 50 words.
I sat at the computer, typed a few words, then
erased them: but nothing came. I drew a little
picture to see if that would help and still nothing
came. Oh! I can write a story in 50 words!

Paul Quixley (12)
King Edward VI Grammar School, Louth

The Crash

He cried, she cried, everyone cried! The ship was closer to the rock. What was going to happen? *Bang! Crash! Boom!* The ship was hit and then sank. Everyone was fighting for survival. People tried climbing out and swimming across the ocean, but died. Any survive . . . ? No, they did not!

Molly Unwin (13)
King Edward VI Grammar School, Louth

The Sweet Shop

The sweet shop was shut, but I tried the door and it opened. I stepped inside and shouted, 'Hello?' but it bounced back at me and echoed. I walked behind the counter. The till swung open. I was starting to worry. I saw something pass in a flash … sweet mystery.

Hannah Charlton (12)

King Edward VI Grammar School, Louth

Alone?

Down the twisting path with the peaceful
meandering river flowing gently alongside. What
a wonderful sight. The sun beaming through the
enormous weeping willows, a gentle breeze from
behind. All alone in the fresh air. But then, all of a
sudden, *plop!* Bill Oddie fell out of an oak tree.

Josh Pinder (13)

King Edward VI Grammar School, Louth

Loneliness

He had lived alone. 'Crazy Bat' we used to call him. Said he murdered anyone in his way. How stupid was I to go see if it was true? Through the tall, dark trees I went. In silence, I entered the house. He was waiting. I was dead. Trapped. Alone.

Abbie Lynch (12)
King Edward VI Grammar School, Louth

Virus

A virus, that's all it took. The virus, the creation of a lunatic named Henry Benill, was created by combining Ebola, Influenza and MRSA. The result was a disease that turned millions into creatures with an IQ barely higher than a goldfish. And so, everyone mutated into ostriches with dyslexia.

David Cliffen (11)

King Edward VI Grammar School, Louth

The Rabid Mouse

The mouse darted left and right as the eagle's eyes homed in on its prey. It swooped and it swooped again, but … *boom!* Shot! The hunter shot the eagle.

Later that day the mouse bit the hunter, giving him rabies. He then went on to kill everyone … then he died.

George Cunningham (12)
King Edward VI Grammar School, Louth

Ghost Town

Sam walked down the street. It was a dank, cold November. A street lamp flicked on. Nobody was about, no shops were open and it wasn't dark. A shop door opened … a dustbin fell over. There was no wind. He went through the door … *Bam!* He wasn't seen again.

James Brown (12)

King Edward VI Grammar School, Louth

73

Unbelievable

Jorge Lorenzo was just about to enter the last corner at Donington and win the race. *Bang!* All of a sudden his bike cut out. Could it be a repeat of last year at Catalunya when he had crashed on the last lap? No, he'd just run out of fuel!

Joshua Grantham (12)

King Edward VI Grammar School, Louth

The Race

The speed picked up. It was lightning now. The
fish caught up. The dolphin looked confused.
Out of nowhere appearing above the water was
a massive mouth of razor-sharp teeth. Too late.
It was a sad end for the dolphin. *Crunch!* As the
mouth closed and enjoyed its feast!

Katie Bath (12)

King Edward VI Grammar School, Louth

75

Alone In The World

It was cold. It was damp. I was alone. All I wanted was to get out and find my family. I knew I couldn't though. If I did, my mum would definitely kill me. Perfect. If only I'd been told how to turn the wretched heating on. Curse this house!

Cian Patrick (12)

King Edward VI Grammar School, Louth

Beth's Magical Dream

It was cold and icy. Beth heard a voice behind her, a sweet and tiny voice. She turned around to see a small creature with wings. 'Who are you?' asked Beth. Its wings fluttered. The creature flew around Beth's head. Beth fell to the ground. With a start she awoke.

Megan Warsap (11)

King Edward VI Grammar School, Louth

Death Near

Elizabeth was running for her life. The shadow of doom was closing in. Liz reached a wall. She was trapped! As the darkness got nearer she trembled. If the darkness even touched her, she would be dead. Suddenly the shadow stopped. It looked at Elizabeth, and the shadow fled! *Why?*

Emily Watts (11)

King Edward VI Grammar School, Louth

The Poor Girl Megan

Once a girl called Megan was walking through the woods. She thought she could hear something, so she looked behind her, banged into a tree and lost her memory.

Five years later she woke up in a brain surgeon's office. She couldn't see properly. Was it all a dream?

Poppy Torrington (11)
King Edward VI Grammar School, Louth

The Great Fire

Animals ran to save their lives as the blaze
approached. Red, yellow and orange. The hot
mass seethed as it chased the inhabitants from
their homes.
A hero, tall and magnificent, came with a machine
that destroyed the blaze, freeing the animals of
the monster that had occupied their homes.

Catherine Hodgetts (11)
Monks Dyke Technology College, Louth

Penguin

'Mum, can I have a Penguin?'
'Yes,' Mum gasped.
It was like she thought I dreamed of them night and day. I crunched into the Penguin. *Mmm,* so delicious, the taste goes right down your throat and lasts forever.

That was a lovely bar of chocolate!

Georgia Harris (11)
Monks Dyke Technology College, Louth

81

Zombies

They chased me. I ran. They surrounded me. So
I shot at them randomly. Sadly resistance was
futile. The zombies ripped my head off.
That was the end of me. *Game over.*
Play again!

Ellis Appleby (11)
Monks Dyke Technology College, Louth

Whoosh!

Should I go up or not? Adrenaline pumping, I
shuffled up!
It was my turn. I took a deep breath, I was off!
Whoosh! Screaming, toppling, falling, upside
down, water up my nose, spinning, spiralling,
down, *splash*, stop! I gradually surfaced gasping
for air, spluttering but smiling.

Lily Megan Alice Watson (12)
Monks Dyke Technology College, Louth

83

A Day In The Woods

One day, me and my family went for a day in the
woods. We all heard a squeal so we investigated.
We saw it was a hurt squirrel, stuck, so we helped
it and put it somewhere safe.
What a day it was, especially the squirrel's.
What a shame!

Courtney Smith (11)
Monks Dyke Technology College, Louth

As Fast As A Car

Racing as fast as a car I sped round the corner. My heart was beating uncontrollably. I took a deep breath, hoping it would last the last few metres until the finish line.
Suddenly I was woken by my mum telling me it was time for breakfast.

Mollie Coney (11)
Monks Dyke Technology College, Louth

85

The Creature

The creature flies through the open window,
landing on the table. Just seeing it makes my
mouth drop open. I back away towards the door.
The creature notices me, spreads its wings and
flies away.
Damn, I was going to take a photo of that
butterfly.

Allana Kaye (11)
Monks Dyke Technology College, Louth

Super Seven

Once upon a time there were seven elves. They had a problem. Santa had gone psycho! He was after all the naughty children. It was down to the seven elves to stop him. Santa was asleep. They had no choice. Goodbye Santa! We'll see you next year!

Carla Kelly (13)
Monks Dyke Technology College, Louth

Fred's Dead

Once upon a future Fred will die! That future is in
five minutes.
He enters the house looming in front of him.
The door slams behind him. 'Hello?' he shouts,
echoing through the house. A whistling sound.
'What's that?' Fred finds out when it hits his head.
Fred's gone, dead!

Kieren Smith (13)
Monks Dyke Technology College, Louth

The Vocation

Dawn breaks, Santa falls out of bed, puts on his
fluffy pink slippers and stomps to the shower. On
goes his shower cap and he washes till he's clean.
He gets into his Santa costume, fake beard and
brown sack.
Another shift in that stuffy grotto listening to
wish lists.

Georgia Murray (14)
Monks Dyke Technology College, Louth

89

The Night Before Christmas

Santa had a busy night ahead so he went to sleep.
Suddenly he was woken with a tickle at his feet.
It was Gilbert, his elf, saying, 'Get up Sleepyhead,
Dasher, Dancer, Prancer, Vixen, Comet, Cupid,
Donna, Blitzen and Rudolph are ready to be fed!

Michael Larsen (13)

Monks Dyke Technology College, Louth

Fright Night

Two girls out in the night, expecting nothing but
a fright. As the distant clock tower chimed, over
the bridge did they climb, only to be faced by one
big fence which made the situation uncomfortably
tense. If only they'd looked or glanced, they
would maybe have stood a chance.

Billie Matchett (14)

Monks Dyke Technology College, Louth

91

The Axe

Her evil eyes watched as me and my friend, Ted,
stood in front of her. Her axe was held tightly in
her muscular hand. She stepped back and raised
her axe high above Ted's head, he screamed as
she brought it towards him …
She stepped back, 'You want some wood?'

Katherine Wain (14)
Monks Dyke Technology College, Louth

My Sister!

I walked carefully into the creepy wooden house.
My friend, Carol, and I were terrified! I thought
I saw someone, I heard something. A ghost! We
followed the noises up the stairs. We ran into the
room, it was my sister trying to scare us!

Lucy Hand (13)
Monks Dyke Technology College, Louth

93

Incy Wincy Spider

Incy Wincy Spider climbed up the window frame.
Down came the hail and ruined the spider's fame.
Out came his mummy and tried to do the same.
Then what happened to Incy, happened all again!

Francesca Wilson (13)
Monks Dyke Technology College, Louth

What Really Happened To Georgy Porgy

Georgy Porgy loved pork pies. Stole one from the butcher and made him cry. When he came out with a knife, he took away Georgy's life. Georgy Porgy lives no more, without him around, it's a bore. Look out for Butcher Man or he will kill you with his pan.

Dani Millthorpe (14)

Monks Dyke Technology College, Louth

The Butcher

Once upon a time, there was a pig who was a butcher. He had customers every day and he even cooked and sold meat to his queen. The pig's most famous, delicious dish, was the one advertised on the sign ...
'Human leg, arm and foot - three for two.'

Keren Newlove (13)
Monks Dyke Technology College, Louth

96

Rudolph

Twisting and turning, he flew through the air. He needed to get to all the houses in time for the morning. In a frantic race against time, he battled through the freezing air. He landed on the last house roof.
In a victory over time, Rudolf started the journey home.

Will East (14)

Monks Dyke Technology College, Louth

97

When Santa Got Stuck Up The Chimney

Santa put on his hat, walked to the sleigh, called
the reindeers' names. Flight began. Children's gifts
were placed under trees. The last house. Looking
rather fat, he tried to get down the chimney.
The next morning, presents opened but no one
noticed the boots sticking out of the fireplace.

Hollie Wilkinson (14)

Monks Dyke Technology College, Louth

The Reindeer

Tonight was the night. I got with my crew and then, *slap!* Off we flew.
First we started in China, then Japan, then England … it was tiring. Whilst he was delivering, a vicious man walked up and said, 'Can I have an autograph?' After that we flew home - fast!

Alex Carter (13)

Monks Dyke Technology College, Louth

99

Alone In The Dark

I thought I was alone. I looked around and saw dark walls of isolation. I went to sit on the only chair there, when somebody tapped my shoulder. I spun around and saw him. Him whom I thought had died. As I cried, he held me close. I wasn't alone!

Chelsea Johnston (13)

Monks Dyke Technology College, Louth

Innocent Life ...

I stepped through the door, and then it struck me,
that poor, innocent life had been taken, battered,
then scalded in a bubbling vat, then after a couple
of seconds, withdrawn. What a way to go ...
'So love, how many fish is it for you?'

Oliver Fairless (13)
Monks Dyke Technology College, Louth

101

Frozen Grass

Frost lingers still on the statue-like grass, solid like a rock. As you take a step, your foot sinks into the needles with a sudden stop where the mud has frozen into a concrete lump. You kick. Steam contracts from it, a crisp rustle evacuates from their speakers.

Courtney Robinson (14)
Monks Dyke Technology College, Louth

Candy Rock

The candy mixture was mixed, the colouring was added, the mix was ready. It got rolled and rolled until it was as thick as a ring. Then, suddenly, *snap!* The rock snapped in two and the words appeared. The rock was too good to share, all of it to myself.

Charlotte Marshall (14)

Monks Dyke Technology College, Louth

103

Prey Vs Predator

Slash! The air whirled like a washing machine, its creator after the helpless deer. The lion's paw pounded on the floor. It tried again but the prey dodged.

Suddenly the lion stopped and hid in the long, wavy grass. The sly lion had seen what the deer hadn't. *Snap!*

Jessica Lynskey (11)

Monks Dyke Technology College, Louth

The Danger Of A Phone Call

The girl got a phone call. It was a stranger. He
wanted her to meet him but wouldn't say his
name. He sounded young so she went. She got
there and there was nobody, until she turned
around.
That girl was never seen again. All because of that
phone call!

Chelsea Gadsby (13)
Monks Dyke Technology College, Louth

Untitled

On the weekend we were putting the Christmas tree up. Ten minutes later my mum got a phone call from the hospital. They said, 'Your son has been run over by a car. He's fine. He would like to see you here now. He's called Robert David Kennard.'

Robert Kennard (13)

Monks Dyke Technology College, Louth

Five Little Pixies

Five pixies walked out of their toadstool. One
pinched Sad's hat. 'Hee hee,' giggled Cheeky. Sad
started to cry,
'It's OK, we will find it,' said Cheery. They looked
all over the toadstool forest.
The four pixies came back and found Cheeky
asleep with Sad's hat covering his face.

Megan Markham (13)
Monks Dyke Technology College, Louth

The Heartbroken Princess

There was a stunning princess who fell in love
with an endearing prince who had to flee to a
battle. He used to write disarming letters to his
love.
One dreary day she didn't get one, he was dead!
She cried seas of bitter tears.

Jade Moncaster (14)
Monks Dyke Technology College, Louth

Little Miss Riding Hood

I was once a little girl on a faraway island.
One day I found a wolf in Grandmother's bed. I
said, *'Ooh,* what big eyes you have, and massive
teeth!' With that I screamed, the wolf jumped up
at me, I screeched at the top of my voice;
he exploded!

Kari Yarsley (15)
Monks Dyke Technology College, Louth

A Day As A Teacher

I step into class, pull out my planner, try to make
the most of the day ahead of me. The classes
I have aren't the best, but one is head and
shoulders above the rest.
The class comes in, great, let the game begin.
'Don't forget your homework, Class.'

Joe Davenport (14)
Monks Dyke Technology College, Louth

A Day Of Life As Santa's Enemy

I'm very busy wrecking Santa's night, trying to wake all the children, giving them a fright. Santa delivers presents, I take them all away, sliding down the chimneys, trying to ruin the future day. I never got presents, I never got treats, all Santa left was coal at my feet.

Ellie Freeman (14)
Monks Dyke Technology College, Louth

The Haunted House

He stared at the haunted house in horror and started to cautiously creep towards the blood-splattered door. Rob slowly opened the door and stared in horror! He could not believe his eyes. The hallway of the supposedly haunted house was filled with McDonald's burgers!
Rob died of McDeath.

Joshua Tunnicliffe (13)
Monks Dyke Technology College, Louth

Flower Power

The seed wiggled deep under the damp soil,
desperate to burst out into a magnificent, bright
yellow sunflower.
Sun beamed down from the highest clouds, whilst
the next day rain poured down. First the stem,
then the leaves began to emerge slowly.
Finally it shared its beauty with the world.

Megan Johnson (11)
Monks Dyke Technology College, Louth

Flat As A Pancake

With a zoom and a rush and with speed, the elephant was racing against the centipede. With a jump, wriggle and a step, the elephant won the race because he was bigger than the centipede. Now the centipede is as flat as a pancake. The elephant stepped on him.

Courtney-Dee Jones (11)
Monks Dyke Technology College, Louth

Stars

The moon shone like a cat's eye glimmering in the night sky. The stars so bright, I tried to count them, but there were too many - hundreds, even thousands.
After minutes, even hours, a shooting star flew by like a cheetah running at the speed of light!
Stars and moon!

Abigail Davies (11)

Monks Dyke Technology College, Louth

Scrooge Of Christmas

'Spoilt children everywhere - to be honest I don't care! One piece of coal is all I got, the decorations I forgot.'
'There goes Scrooge again!' Scrooge was walking past. *'Ooh,* please Sir, any crust of bread for those in need?'
Scrooge gave a grunt. What a horrible man indeed!

Carla-Libby Ervin (12)
Monks Dyke Technology College, Louth

Zombie

There once was a girl called Little Pink Riding
Hood who had a machine gun.
One day she was taking a walk when a zombie
stopped her and said, 'Erber!'
She ran off. The zombie chased her, so she shot it
in the face and went home to Mum.

Macaulay Douglas (13)
Monks Dyke Technology College, Louth

Untitled

The girl was expecting loads of presents on Christmas Day She woke up and she was so sad to see that her present was not a lot. She looked over, and her brother and sister had quite a lot so that wrecked her Christmas that year.

Hannah Dixon (13)

Monks Dyke Technology College, Louth

Santa Baby!

'Santa Baby, hurry down the chimney tonight!'
sang Maisie, who was supposed to be in bed!
She knew Santa wouldn't come if she was
naughty. She finally got to sleep then woke up,
her stocking was empty! Maisie didn't get any
presents that year, but she was never naughty
again.

Maisie Goulsbra

Monks Dyke Technology College, Louth

119

The Wish

On a school trip to Paris we were all telling jokes;
nobody laughed at mine, but minutes later it
got told again and everyone laughed. Chloe just
laughed at me! How rude!
Suddenly the boat started to sink … !
Be careful what you wish for!

Gabrielle Murray (12)
Monks Dyke Technology College, Louth

The Dog

Bella's mum had gone out Christmas shopping.
When Bella got scared, she put her hand down
for the dog to lick. She heard some clanging
chains.
An hour later she went to the toilet, the dog had
been hung!
The question was, what was licking her hand for
that hour?

Poppy-Rose Jenner (11)
Monks Dyke Technology College, Louth

Goldilocks

Goldilocks strolled through the beautiful forest.
She came to Bears' house. She caught sight of
their porridge cooling on the table. Baby Bear's
porridge was perfect! Goldilocks splintered his
chair accidentally then instantly fell asleep
on his bed.
Suddenly the three bears returned and saw
Goldilocks through the upstairs window …

Alice Cliffen (11)
Monks Dyke Technology College, Louth

Poppy's Last Day!

Poppy was an extraordinarily strange girl! One day she was strolling along, suddenly she heard a pop and her nail blew off, then all her nails blew off. Next, she was getting bigger and bigger until she was lifted off the ground!
That was the end of Poppy!

Jessica Des-Forges (11)
Monks Dyke Technology College, Louth

The Forest

I dreamt horrific pictures of me running through the forest in my pjs and bare feet. I woke up in distress until I realised it was only a nightmare, but my feet were muddy, sore. I was confused. Was it true and what was I running that fast from?

Ashleah Wright (12)
Monks Dyke Technology College, Louth

Night Terrors

I was sprinting through the forest as fast as I
could, the branches were lashing against my face.
I could feel blood trickling down my cheek. The
only thing I knew was that I was running from
someone or something. I tripped over, I saw the
ghostly silhouette facing me …

Elliot Jennings (11)

Monks Dyke Technology College, Louth

The Muddy Pig!

Elle was a spoilt child who lived on a farm. She woke up one crisp morning and her pig had eight piglets. To her surprise, one of them wouldn't go in mud! Unusual for pigs!
So Elle ordered four wellies to be specially made for Porkers.

Lauren Tindall (11)
Monks Dyke Technology College, Louth

Sheepy

Once upon a time there was a black sheep who was hairy and scary and had to be sheared. He gave a bag to the farmer's wife and two bags to the little boy who visited the farm every day. But one day he didn't come to the farm …

Tristan Roantree (11)

Monks Dyke Technology College, Louth

The Ogre!

Crystal went running down a long, dark alley. A spooky shadow appeared over her. A shiver went down her bony spine. It was a big, fat, hairy ogre! *'Argh'* screamed Crystal. By the time she got out the damp alley, she realised that the ogre was her gran's new boyfriend!

Natalie Stainton (12)

Monks Dyke Technology College, Louth

The Bike

Once there was a man called Mike who decided
to fall off his bike. He let out a shriek and began
to leak. He tried to fix his bike, but was an
absolutely useless mechanic, so he decided to
walk.

Jessica Holness (14)
Monks Dyke Technology College, Louth

Eddie The Elephant

There was a baby elephant called Eddie. He was much bigger than his friends. They were scared of him. One day, Eddie heard a squeaking from the river. Investigating, he found little Mousey drowning. Eddie gently scooped him up and carried him back. From then on he was a hero!

Emily Castledine (15)

Monks Dyke Technology College, Louth

130

Tiger Hears A Rumour

One day a talking tiger heard a rumour that tigers were going to become extinct. The tiger waddled on its hind legs to a human and asked politely whether this rumour was true. The human screamed and ran away. So the tiger asked another human and the same thing happened.

Emma Kirkby (11)

Monks Dyke Technology College, Louth

When Time Began

When the world first existed, dinosaurs ruled the
land. But one day, one thing changed everything.
That one thing started the human race.
Thousands of years later religious races and
ethnic tribes began. That led to a new era of
human life.
In the modern day, technology is the era.

Nick Howman

Monks Dyke Technology College, Louth

The Radio

You are waiting at the traffic lights. You turn the radio on. The crackling of someone's voice as they try to talk to you. The lights turn amber and then green. You move, but there's still no sound. As you move away from the lights, the voice comes alive.

Sophie Brown (14)

Monks Dyke Technology College, Louth

Untitled

I was trembling with fear as it was my first time on a roller coaster. I stepped on the contraption. Everyone else had smiles on their faces whilst I had fear and shock on my face. It started! Before I knew it, it was over and I was happy again.

Carl Rushby

Monks Dyke Technology College, Louth

Danger Alone

Falling rocks. In the middle of nowhere, far away from civilisation. Tearing rope. Going down the face of the mountain. *Argh!* A cave-storm's coming. *Brrr!* It's getting cold. Blizzard winds. Sat in my cave with no one with me except myself. Death staring at me. Now what?

George Benson (15)

Monks Dyke Technology College, Louth

Alone

Their cold breath filled the air. They were alone in the early hours of the morning. A shadow lurked behind them. Slowly the couple turned around to see what was behind them. There was a loud bang. They ran. A car had backfired.

Ian Heggie

Monks Dyke Technology College, Louth

Terror Dentist

Went to the dentist last week. Sat there all nervous. Really didn't want to go to get a filling. I was sat squeezing my boyfriend's hand saying, 'I don't want to go!'
Then they came and got me. Heart pounding, I just forgot about the pain and just did it.

Molly Keningale
Monks Dyke Technology College, Louth

Painful

I was in the doctor's waiting for my jab. I could hear the music playing in the background. Then the nurse came into the waiting room and told me to come through.
I sat down and closed my eyes and it was all over!
I walked out rubbing my arm.

Kara Trench

Monks Dyke Technology College, Louth

Christiana And The Toad

Christiana was walking in the swamp. She was lost. She saw a small, slimy toad. 'Please help me get home,' yelped Christiana. So the toad took her home. She reached down for a kiss. As her red lips touched his, she turned into a toad. Now they are both happy.

Gemma Mendham (12)

Monks Dyke Technology College, Louth

Rosie Red Has Wrecked Christmas!

Rosie was a girl with red hair. One day Rosie went shopping for Christmas presents for her mum but she couldn't decide what to buy. So she closed her eyes and picked something randomly!
On Christmas Day, Rosie's mum ended up getting men's shaving foam!
'Rosie!' yelled her angry mother.

Steven Hallgarth-McGhee (11)

Monks Dyke Technology College, Louth

Big Blue Walking Hood

Amanda was kind, so she went to take food to her ill granny. She went through the forest, she saw Mr Chicken. He was evil. As she carried on through the humid forest, she got to her granny's. The door was unlocked, there was a noise. *'Argh!'* she screamed, *'help!'*

Laura Barber (11)

Monks Dyke Technology College, Louth

141

The Slug And The Ferret

One bright, sunny day, a little ferret named Fred
was strolling through a forest when he met a
hoodie slug. The thug slug wanted his money, but
Fred was eating a bag of 'salt and shake' crisps
and hadn't used the salt. This was what the slug
got!

Hollie Vessey (12)
Monks Dyke Technology College, Louth

Rapunzel

There was a girl with long blonde hair. She lived
with an ugly witch.
One day the witch decided to lock her up in a
mangy old tower with only one window!
A prince came past and saw Rapunzel, so he
climbed up the tower and later they got married.

Joanne Broughton (12)
Monks Dyke Technology College, Louth

Kidnapped

A scabby, dry hand squeezed her mouth to stifle
the high-pitched scream from the young, tender
girl. Her limbs wrenched with rope, cutting off
circulation …
Drowsy and drugged she woke up in the
spotlight. Filthy, putrid men bid on her … *Sold!*
A cold, stale, white hand grabbed her…

Jeremy Hall (12)

Monks Dyke Technology College, Louth

Pippy's Poppy

Pippy had a poppy. Pippy loved her poppy. One day Pippy went out into the garden. It was gone! She looked everywhere for her poppy. Under a pot in the garage. Everywhere! It was gone. Suddenly, when she looked up she saw it was there.
Pippy loved her poppy.

Hayley Holmquest (11)
Monks Dyke Technology College, Louth

145

Ghost!

The hall was dark and silent, not a creature was stirring, but then, suddenly, as the head teacher was locking up, he heard a door slam. *What was it? Who could it be?* All sorts of thoughts were running through his head.
He felt a knife in his back. Dead!

Sam Wilson (13)

Monks Dyke Technology College, Louth

Snowy Sleigh Day

It was Christmas Day, Tim and Tom opened their present. It was a sleigh! They dashed out the door and flew down the hill on the sleigh. They crashed into the snow. 'Tim, we're snowmen!' Tom laughed, swimming out of the snow. They jumped out of the snow and laughed!

Sophie Barker (12)

Monks Dyke Technology College, Louth

Little Red Riding Hood!

One day a young girl was skipping through the village singing, 'La, la, la.' She suddenly stopped and looked up at a dark shadow. There stood a huge, scary wolf breathing in her face. She dropped everything and ran. The wolf chased her into a trap but she got away.

Chloe Offer (12)

Monks Dyke Technology College, Louth

Santa's Stuck

Santa was jammed up the chimney, his belly full of mince pies, 'You girls and boys, come heave me out or there'll be no presents tonight.' The children yanked Santa out whilst dragging sacks of presents too.
Christmas Eve with Santa Claus, Rudolph and mince pies. A night to remember!

Kieren Dales (12)
Monks Dyke Technology College, Louth

Bandslam: The Final Jam

Sam and her band stood nervously backstage. 'Alright, this is it, let's go blow their socks off!' she said, encouragingly. They were one minute away from their biggest performance *ever!* Thirty seconds. The last minute nerves kicked in. 'I can't do this,' said Macy, but they'd already walked onstage.

Laura-Mae Ferrier (12)
Monks Dyke Technology College, Louth

The Highwayman

A shadow emerged in the darkness, the pistols in his hands. Tied up, the poor fair maiden, just one life need he end. He waited at the shutters for his suspect, when he heard the gunshot roar.
The poor fair maiden's suicide was the last thing that horrid man saw.

Megan Millson (13)
Monks Dyke Technology College, Louth

Clown

Emma and Silver went on a ghost train at Skegness. When they were on it, they got really scared when they saw a clown at the back of them.

When the ride was over, they weren't there! A man went in and found them, but there was no clown.

Sarah Winn (13)

Monks Dyke Technology College, Louth

Winter Wonder Weird

Jimmy stood waiting, 'It's gonna snow, I hope it
does because Christmas hasn't been the same
since Mum died.' He was ecstatic. It hadn't
snowed for years. 'Don't get too excited!'
He counted to twelve. *It won't snow,* but it did and
Jimmy swore he saw his mum that day.

Bethany Tindall (13)
Monks Dyke Technology College, Louth

153

Unkind Act

Once upon a time there was an antisocial
chavette called Holly.
One morning her mum said, 'Go see your sick
nan.'
Holly replied, 'No!' She lit her cigarette and began
to totally ignore her mum. When her mum finally
had enough, she went to see her mum herself.

Sarah Briggs (12)
Monks Dyke Technology College, Louth

A New Assignment

Tom crept through the office block silently.
He needed to grab the documents and get
out. No guards alerted. No bloodshed. The
documents were in sight, but two guards were
guarding them. He drew his pistol and with two
shots, disposed of them both. He snatched the
documents.
Training over.

James Price (12)

Monks Dyke Technology College, Louth

155

The Assassin

I swung at his face with my bare fist. He lashed at me with his foot. I grabbed something hard, the only loose thing in the dark alley. An iron pipe! I slammed it into his neck with all my might. Blood flew, I stared, fists clenched.
I'd killed him …

Aimee Wright (12)
Queen Elizabeth's Grammar School, Alford

Suicide Kid

I felt it press my head … *click!*
This is how it goes. It was a normal morning,
he was at it already: verbal, physical, cyber - all
the time. I was too scared to tell - I became a
shadow. That night I got the ornamental gun and
killed myself. Suicide Kid.

Lucy Thompson (12)
Queen Elizabeth's Grammar School, Alford

Young Killer

With a knife in one hand, a body in the other, the boy crept along a path in a dark tunnel. At the end was a sewer, he put the body into it along with the knife. What he didn't notice was that there was a policeman behind him.
Busted!

Sarah-Jane Price (11)

Queen Elizabeth's Grammar School, Alford

A Dog's Life

I stroke Lia with my eyes shut, and wonder what
it would be like to be a dog …
Smells tingle in my nose. Opening my eyes widely,
I see someone near me. I try to speak, but it
comes out as a bark.
I wish I were human …

Juliette Bretan (12)
Queen Elizabeth's Grammar School, Alford

159

Fighting Joey

Albert's father came home on market day, drunk.
He came back with young colt, Joey. Albert
trained Joey to be a beautiful farm horse.
Albert was in bed one night and nobody knew,
but Albert's father was taking Joey to be sold to a
caring man from the army.

Lucy Bowles (12)

Queen Elizabeth's Grammar School, Alford

The Grey Lady

A manor house stood, and a family of husband,
wife and daughter lived inside. That night the lady
was with her daughter alone. There were bangs
on the door. She went to answer it. Her husband
was dead!
She ran to find a knife. She raised it, and killed
herself!

Daisy Blair (13)
Queen Elizabeth's Grammar School, Alford

161

Too Greedy For Her Own Good

'Three double-decker ice creams,' Betty slurred.
'Sorry, ran out.' said the man.
She hit him. He flew backwards. She left the ice
cream man thinking of something evil.
The next day he gave her poisoned ice cream and
she died of extreme stomach cramps and
a heart attack.

Colette Dewick-Elsele (13)
Queen Elizabeth's Grammar School, Alford

Water Torture

Water. Drowning. Can't breathe. I tried to sit up
and failed. Someone with strong arms, the kind
you get from bodybuilding, was holding me down
under this murky black water that was creeping
into my lungs! *Can't breathe. I'm gonna drown.*
Then the worst possible thought hit me.
Blackness.

Jessica Ann Cunningham (13)
Queen Elizabeth's Grammar School, Alford

Twist In The Tale

The bitter wind was howling around the
mountain, threatening to pull Lynette and Amelie
off at any moment, ruining their climb for charity.
There was a sudden crunch as a large boulder
came tumbling down, only just missing Lynette.
'Cut!'
The foam rock bounced off the floor of the set.

Katie Walker (12)
Queen Elizabeth's Grammar School, Alford

The Shadow!

Tommy plodded upstairs. He went into the
bathroom and brushed his teeth. He saw a
creamy brown tail. He cautiously crept to his
bedroom. He sat up, bolt upright, and slowly
scanned his small room. His eyes darted towards
the door. His mother came in, she smiled, 'It's
only Kitty!'

Maisie Epton (12)

Queen Elizabeth's Grammar School, Alford

The Bus

Me and Jessica went to Skegness for a day. We woke up and walked to the bus stop. The bus arrived and we sat down for a fun journey. Jess was not there. My head was full of screams. I could nearly smell the blood. It turned dark and silent.

Ellie Winter (12)

Queen Elizabeth's Grammar School, Alford

War

I smashed through a house. That civilian would be
killed by the pursuers easily. I climbed up a ladder.
A helicopter flew above me.
Boom! the helicopter was hit, it spun, people fell
out, I dived to the lower rooftop. Some bullets
missed me.
Down the helicopter came, onto me …

Joshua Padgett (12)
Queen Elizabeth's Grammar School, Alford

On Borrowed Time ...

Ouch! There it goes. *Ouch!* and again. It's annoying
now! I'm helped onto a helicopter. '1, 2, *lift!'*
Onto the bed I go. 'Blood pressure critical!' I hear
the doctor. It can't be that bad. I only got hit on
the head.
Beep! I drifted into a deep, deep sleep ...

Chloe Marston (13)
Queen Elizabeth's Grammar School, Alford

The Dream

I opened a door and started falling. I wanted to re-enter my life but my body was no more. I was crushed. Suddenly, I stopped falling and walked towards another door. I couldn't tell if it was light or dark. Then a voice said, 'Time to go to school.'

Daniel Grummitt (13)
Queen Elizabeth's Grammar School, Alford

Meating Of Mind!

'Mum! There's a hole in my meatball!'
'What?'
'My meatball has a hole in it!' Suddenly mini
meatballs came charging out of the centre! *'Eek!'*
'Vie are zie meaty meatballs!'
'Why you here?'
'Vie want you to join our army!'
'Well, *erm,* I don't know, I'll ask my mum! 'Mum!'

Stefan Evans (12)
Queen Elizabeth's Grammar School, Alford

The Thrill

I screamed, it threw me up, turned me upside down. A skeleton touched my face. My heart jumped through some goo, I saw bloody images of myself, they started walking towards me. I slipped over and got off the roller coaster. I awoke, not realising it was a bad dream.

Connor Stephen (12)

Queen Elizabeth's Grammar School, Alford

The Bonfire That Went Wrong

Young Kate lived in a mansion with her family.
They had a bonfire party with friends and family.
Kate was wandering round the fire and fell in.
Burned. Melted. Scorched. The fire killed her!
Her whole family and all the friends rushed
frantically to the screams, it was too late.

Jessica Morris (12)
Queen Elizabeth's Grammar School, Alford

Michael's Afro

One day Michael went for a walk in the park. A
ferocious dog jumped into his hair. He had to go
and get his hair cut off. He went to 'Fellas'. His
hair fell off, the puppy jumped out and they both
ran away. He found it in the bin.

Michael Rothery (12)
Queen Elizabeth's Grammar School, Alford

Forever Changing

It's happening. The pain's writhing through my human body. Bold black hairs sprout over me. Bat-like wings morph from my arms. Yellow fangs replace my teeth. I scream. I have a long black tail. Why am I cursed? Why am I a killing monster? I scream. Only a dream.

Rachel Brook (13)
Queen Elizabeth's Grammar School, Alford

Dying Moments

I've been in hospital for ages. I'm dying, alone. My
life's disappearing. It could be minutes, seconds.
Someone appears. 'Hello?'
I gasp. 'Mum!' My eyes close. My best day ever.
Beeeep! My last minute, second.
My first smile. This is what happiness feels like.
I shall stay like this forever.

Chloe Johnson (12)
Queen Elizabeth's Grammar School, Alford

Silhouetted Dreams

The street was empty, illuminated by a single light. Sitting on a park bench was Joe McDuff, a prehistorically old man. Next to the bench was a silhouetted figure. Joe turned around and saw the figure, he ran like a sports car. The figure chased him. *Wham!* Joe woke up!

Liam Clough (12)
Queen Elizabeth's Grammar School, Alford

The Beast

Sprinting, Jake's clothes were tearing on the brambles. He'd been running since his father accidentally discovered the green liquid. His father gave him a vial containing it. Now, he was being chased. Thorns were piercing his skin. He tripped and fell, turning over.
Blood-red eyes were staring at him.

Joseph Lynch (12)
Queen Elizabeth's Grammar School, Alford

177

The Abbey

Joe, Seb and Kyle ran towards the derelict abbey through the moonlit garden. Seb walked towards the abbey's ornate door. He put his hand on the cold, stiff knob and twisted. It was hard and difficult to move. Seb walked inside. He heard something move behind him.
He turned around …

James Spence (13)
Queen Elizabeth's Grammar School, Alford

Danger

I fell and I was being watched. I rushed up a tree
and fell asleep. I went into a desert and found
myself before a large lizard. I attacked it and
threw it at an old tree. I saw a small salamander.
It showed me a hole in a tree.

Eleanor Crome (12)
Queen Elizabeth's Grammar School, Alford

Green-Eyed Girl

Niagra met me at the huge medieval door. Inside,
duvets spilled awkwardly over bumps in the bed.
Just then, in the far corner, a beautiful brunette
rose gracefully, her long hair to her waist and
framing her bright green eyes perfectly. She
yawned softly and stretched her big white wings.

Summer Furniss (12)

Queen Elizabeth's Grammar School, Alford

180

The House

I enter. Instantly I can smell rotting wood. Then
I see them. They're watching television. They
shoot through the roof and a murderous black
smoke appears! I stumble up the stairs but my
exit is blocked. I look back and there's the smoke.
I'm trapped! The ghosts have me now!

Jack Moore (13)

Queen Elizabeth's Grammar School, Alford

The Teller

On planet one … Jim and Bob visit a fortune
teller. The teller says, 'Prepare for planetary war.'
They don't believe her and go on holiday.
After the holiday they enter their house and fall
unconscious. They awake and are trapped. They
escape but they get killed by the aliens.

Ben David Edwards (12)
Queen Elizabeth's Grammar School, Alford

The Disaster

A spaceship was launched into the sky for its next
mission.
Hours later it arrived at its destination, where a
war was taking place.
Soon after the war ended, the small but fast
spaceship left to go back to Earth, but ships
attacked them and they crash-landed to Earth.

Jason Hiew (12)
Queen Elizabeth's Grammar School, Alford

Overseas

The waves were rough and yet the skies were blue, the horizon was sure the homeland was bound. But those beautiful lochs were definitely not.
Boom! Boom! Boom! Down she went, deeper and deeper until she hit the bottom.
As for the crew, well of course they followed too.

Aarron Smith (11)

Queen Elizabeth's High School, Gainsborough

A Bad Relationship

Sometimes I'm too harsh with you and you just
snap back at me. Normally I get annoyed and
chew your head off, then regret it later.
Weeks after trying hard together, the one small
tear blows it all away. I just can't help it! I have to
chew my fingernails.

Alice Walton (12)
Queen Elizabeth's High School, Gainsborough

The Snowy Death

I walked through the graveyard, the snow falling on my head like icing sugar. I had to give Grandpa his present.

What was that? Something behind me. I clung onto the present. I ran, trying to hide behind the gravestone. I looked, only to find a dark figure breathing heavily.

Martha Cottam (11)

Queen Elizabeth's High School, Gainsborough

Back From Afghanistan

My story is of death and horror … We came out
of the pit, we were told it was safe! We walked
far and wide! I heard the words … 'Ambush!'
I was shot in the leg and I saw my team die.
So did my heart. I was the only survivor.

James Denning (11)
Queen Elizabeth's High School, Gainsborough

Ninja Vs Demon

A firestorm raged in the sky as Ninja sped across the rooftops to the ninja dojo. A demon jumped out of the shadows and suddenly offered Ninja a cup of tea and a biscuit.
When they had finished, they started to fight. Ninja finally killed Demon but it was tough.

Joshua Butler (11)
Queen Elizabeth's High School, Gainsborough

Zombunny Vs Super Bunny

It was a time of darkness in Bunny Land. The evil Zombunny was the villain. Nobody liked him now. For one thing he went round going 'Brians! Brians!' because he couldn't spell. So Super Bunny went to give him a spelling lesson. Now Zombunny says, 'Brains' properly. People liked him now.

Elliott Clark (11)

Queen Elizabeth's High School, Gainsborough

189

The Undermarket

The Devil's baby son cried and cried, he wanted
his diapers changing, but the Underlord was
out. The Devil drove to the Undermarket in his
Lamborghini. He walked in. The prices rocketed!
He walked to the nappies, picked up a packet of
Pampers and paid on his *'deadit'* card!

Connor Shaw (12)

Queen Elizabeth's High School, Gainsborough

Ouch!

Today the first Amarillo landed on the moon.
'Houston? Houston? We have encountered a
problem … hailstones are coming … Houston?'
'Amarillo 1-2-3? Our connection is breaking up …'
Squeak!
Amarillo 1-2-3 wandered alone and looked into
space … Hailstones fell heavily. Tears fell from
Amarillo's eyes … *How bad,* he sadly thought …

Alex Noble (11)
Queen Elizabeth's High School, Gainsborough

Mother Nature Can Kill

Lancelot walked out of the B&B and looked at the hurricane. It was a monster (probably sent by that really ugly witch, Morgan, ie Fay). Lancelot ran … and … ran … and ran. He stopped at a pub to refill. The pub was destroyed. Lancelot died.

Jamie Howe (12)

Queen Elizabeth's High School, Gainsborough

The Start Of The End

Bumblebee was in the graveyard waiting for the others. Suddenly there was a slash of lightning and the telephone mast fell down. Then the others turned up, they pushed Bumblebee out of the way and he fell on the tomb of Megatron.
This was the start of the *end!*

Kieran Crawford (12)
Queen Elizabeth's High School, Gainsborough

193

Radioactive Wednesday

On our prolonged journey to America, me and
my dad, Peter, waited for the flight to end. When
we landed, we were asked to stay inside because
there was a big, raging tornado.
Suddenly, a green, sharp, luminous object flew
against the window.
Smash!

Thomas Cox

Queen Elizabeth's High School, Gainsborough

Danger In The Woods

In the distance Sam could see Bella, with Daniel
circulating around her. His eyes were bulging
red with hunger. Sam suddenly started sprinting
towards Bella, changing into his werewolf form.
The pack darted after Sam, helping to destroy
Daniel, knowing that Sam wouldn't be satisfied
until they watched his death.

Darci Vivian (12)

Queen Elizabeth's High School, Gainsborough

The Wolf

He was on the prowl, you could tell, through the air. It was a hot night in the empty girls' school. I was following him, almost stalking him. It was deadly serious business trying to keep up, and still keeping cover. Then he turned - and I knew it was over.

Sarah Lodder-Manning (11)
Queen Elizabeth's High School, Gainsborough

I Can Do It

What was it? It was waiting for me at the end of
the swimming pool. Then it would snatch me and
gobble me up. I was sure of it. *Just keep swimming,*
I told myself. *Just keep swimming, just swim!*
I made it. I showed that monster who was boss!

Rebecca Codd (12)
Queen Elizabeth's High School, Gainsborough

Shot In The Dark

The galloping horse reached the haunted castle.
The clock had ticked midnight. He had followed
his master's directions. 'Steady on.' The owner
had looked up into the castle window. There
stood a man. He was staring at them.
The master got off his horse and walked towards
the castle. *Boom!*

Amelia Priest (12)

Queen Elizabeth's High School, Gainsborough

A Kiss Of Death

The mist hung over the sea like a coat hanging on a washing line. Legend has it that a vampire lives on this very beach. I don't believe it though. People say it comes out on a night much like tonight.

What was that? I heard something behind me …

'Argh!'

Lauren Wilson (11)

Queen Elizabeth's High School, Gainsborough

199

Down

It was too stormy to see, but I knew he was there. The man ran at me, I dodged, then slipped. Soon I was falling deep into the murky depths of the freezing river. His ice-cold hands holding me down. Why couldn't he hear me screaming? Why couldn't he?

Emma Morley (11)
Queen Elizabeth's High School, Gainsborough

The Fox

A twig cracked, leaves rustled, pale, eerie
moonlight filtered through the tree canopy onto
the forest floor. A fox, sleek and elegant, tiptoed
from the undergrowth. The moonlight illuminated
its fur, the shade of polished copper.
Suddenly a bush shook, the fox looked up and
fled away into the darkness.

Elspeth Rider (11)
Queen Elizabeth's High School, Gainsborough

The School Trip

On a bright, sunny day in New York, there
walked a lovely, pretty girl. The reason she was
there was she was on a trip with school.
They were at the Statue of Liberty, when it came
tumbling down upon her. Nobody looked after
her, she was left to die!

Amelia Jane Waterhouse (12)

Queen Elizabeth's High School, Gainsborough

Cinderella Gone Bad

Cinderella was in London. It was midnight and she
was on her way home. The fairy godmother had
told her to be back by this time or her designer
jeans, boots and hoodie would disappear.
Lately she'd gone from gowns to jeans, balls to
nightclubs.
Suddenly the clock struck midnight.

Madaleine Schofield (11)
Queen Elizabeth's High School, Gainsborough

The Dungeons

There, before him was his relatives' home in
Lincoln Castle dungeons. He howled, 'Hello!' It
echoed around the stone cells. *Hello! Hello! Hello!*
Then, in reply … 'Here, darling.' Again it echoed,
Here darling! Here darling! Here darling!
He drifted towards where the sound came from.
'Hello darling, Samuel Sugarbones.'

Elizabeth Booth (11)
Queen Elizabeth's High School, Gainsborough

Bang! Bang! Bang!

Billy awoke in the middle of the night. *Bang! Bang! Bang!* Someone was trying to break in! Billy ran to the kitchen and grabbed the shotgun, scuttled to the door and very slightly pulled the trigger and

…

'What have I told you about playing with that?' his father asked anxiously.

Mackenzie Taylor (11)

Queen Elizabeth's High School, Gainsborough

205

Princess At The Zoo!

It was a lovely sunny day round about lunchtime
and Princess Peach was having a wonderful time
at the nearby zoo! 'Oh my! What a wonderful
zoo,' said the princess as she stroked the animals.
'My favourite animals are the monkeys,' said the
princess. 'They are better than the prince!'

Robyn Steeper (12)
Queen Elizabeth's High School, Gainsborough

I'm A Celeb, Get Me Out Of Here!

One day the amazing Calum Cawkwell was
playing his electric guitar when it came, yes, *it!*
'I'm a celeb, get me out of here.'
'So if you want to keep your favourite in, then
please ring!'
Then Ant and Dec came to say who was going …
'It's you, Calum.'

Elspeth Gray (11)
Queen Elizabeth's High School, Gainsborough

Billy And The Worm

Once Billy was walking in the long, busy streets
of New York. He came across a worm. He was
about to tread on him when he saw the worm
was waving a white flag for mercy.
So Billy threw him in the river and Billy got hit
by lightning.

Ryan Webb (11)
Queen Elizabeth's High School, Gainsborough

Leprechaun Land

The small leprechaun was running through the
forest, dodging every tree in his path. He did
not stop sprinting, he didn't look back. Then, he
finally saw it, the end of the rainbow.
At the end of the rainbow he saw it, his own pot
of gold, just to himself!

Daniel Waters (14)

The Grammar School at Leeds, Leeds

209

Blitz

Last night I had been working on the docks. It was the night of the blitz. London was pretty messed up. A plane had crashed onto the ship I was working on. She went down in a matter of minutes.

My friend's last words were, 'Jim, Jim.'
His pet penguin.

Alistair Howarth (12)
The Grammar School at Leeds, Leeds

Tick-Tock

I start to sweat. Time's almost up. Of course
there are two ways that this could go down. One:
I cut the right wire and go home or two: I run out
of time and I'll never see sunrise again.
I cut the wire, wait … and I live.

Vivek Premraj (13)
The Grammar School at Leeds, Leeds

The Christmas Poltergeist

Once there was a boy called Henry. One holiday,
Henry went away. How unlucky Henry was.
In the cottage where he stayed, a Christmas
poltergeist attacked. All that was left, blood and
bones.
His mother fled but she could not escape and her
body was found floating in a lake.

James Micklethwaite (12)
The Grammar School at Leeds, Leeds

The Invasion

He had the information that I needed to stop the invasion. He entered the warehouse where it all started. After pausing, I decided to go in. He charged into a room, it was pitch-black. Suddenly I thought I had caught him but then they came in from all corners …

Gerard Ellis (12)

The Grammar School at Leeds, Leeds

Swimming

I woke up in a fancy hotel. I looked around and
saw a person who looked like a coach. He looked
at me and said, 'Alright, you're swimming in the
Olympics 200m against Michael Phelps.'
In the last heat, Phelps was ahead. I caught up,
I was ahead and ...

Will Stevenson (12)
The Grammar School at Leeds, Leeds

End Of The World?

I was walking down the road when it started. The
vibrations. The ground started shaking. Since then
it hasn't stopped.
Now I'm at home. My eyes glued to the news.
Bits of china now coming away. I feel the shaking
grow as we go up …

Matthew Walker (12)

The Grammar School at Leeds, Leeds

The Sea

Once upon a time there was a boy called Sam and he lived near the sea. He went to the seaside and into the sea. He got nipped by a crab, bitten by a prawn then drowned slowly and that was the end of Sam.

Benjamin Marks (12)
The Grammar School at Leeds, Leeds

I Don't Like Monday

A girl walked into school. She had a gun. She wasn't sweating or nervous; but she felt strange. It was Monday, she hated Mondays. Her blood pressure suddenly rose and she pulled out the gun. She fired. There were screams. The girl realised what she had done and shot herself.

Tom Gorman (12)

The Grammar School at Leeds, Leeds

The Chase

The woods were covered in blood. It was getting
closer and closer. The rough ground passed under
my feet, sweat dripped from my face. I could
almost feel its putrid breath. Closer and closer it
came. I was slowing down. Suddenly I fell.
The beast had found its prey …

Guiorgi Smith (12)
The Grammar School at Leeds, Leeds

Big Boris Johnson

Boris Johnson's plan for the Olympics is a brilliant plan. The torch will go out, Gordon Brown will cry, Boris will go in thongs looking for a lighter to relight the torch. Chavs will threaten an old lady and our saviour, Big Boris, will shout, '*Oi*, clear off you oinks!'

Matthew Birch (13)
The Grammar School at Leeds, Leeds

A Day At Grizzly Meadow

A rabbit looked at the meadow. It hopped out
and nibbled the grass. The farmer aimed his gun
at the rabbit. The rabbit heard him and bolted.
The farmer took a shot at him. He missed. A big
grizzly bear came and ate the farmer.
The rabbits had a party.

Tom Miller (13)
The Grammar School at Leeds, Leeds

Getting Her Life Back

Tears streamed down her face. The background buzz of the corridor in her ears. The doctor bent down and squeezed her shoulders. The sympathetic nods from waiting patients. But they misunderstood. These were tears of joy. The cancer had gone and she could only stutter three words:

'Thank you, Doctor!'

Lily Megson (16)
The Grammar School at Leeds, Leeds

221

A Walk In The Forest

Snow covered the woods. Nick walked. Then, tracks in the snow. He stopped, followed the prints. All around the pines were silent. The tracks stopped. Before him was a body lying in the snow.
Nick slowly unholstered his rifle. He crouched. Soon snow again began to fall. Nick walked on.

David Woods (16)

The Grammar School at Leeds, Leeds

Untitled

A beam of bright light shone through the window
and a woman could be seen rocking to and fro in
front of a comforting, gleaming fire. There was no
colour in her eyes, they were grieving, grieving
the 100th soldier who died in the gripping war.
Grieving her courageous son.

Aisha Chipampe (16)

The Grammar School at Leeds, Leeds

White

The climber, perched precariously on the cliff edge, was buffeted by the wind and snow as it swirled down from the mountaintop. He stopped. Turned. Heard the distant drums of death as the avalanche came into view and was engulfed by its rushing whiteness. Silence.
The mountain claims another.

Ian Jordan (17)
The Grammar School at Leeds, Leeds

Water Kills

Fiercely ferocious waves engulf her. They slam her down onto the lonely sea floor. She struggles quickly up, fighting and gulping for last breath. Nobody sees. A life ends as several hopeless bubbles float to the ocean surface. She sinks between layers of hungry, icy water and finally, there's peace.

Hannah Myerson (16)

The Grammar School at Leeds, Leeds

Tomorrow?

It was icy-cold. Rain was pelting down. The unforgiving wind hurled ferociously. And there she was. A doll-like toddler with auburn hair and red rosy cheeks. Alone. Afraid. Searching; searching for her mother whilst busy figures brushed violently past her.
In one instant she was gone. Gone forever.

Victoria Scrase (16)

The Grammar School at Leeds, Leeds

Creeper

'Twas a dark night whilst the rain fell. Something crept across the damp ground, leaving slime in its wake. The rain washed away the slime, leaving the ground blank and unmarked.
An untraceable killer that crawls its way to you silently. Your screams fill the night with an unbearable terror.

Emma Russell

Whitcliffe Mount School, Cleckheaton

Life Of War

Bang! The trench became engulfed in smoke,
men coughed and spat blood. Brave, courageous
soldiers fell, others screamed as gas filled their
lungs and started to devour their insides.
Over the treacherous barbed wire came a hoard
of German soldiers. They opened fire, mercifully
killing all in their path.

Matthew Deighton (13)

Whitcliffe Mount School, Cleckheaton

Dead End

It happened on Dead End Street. He was walking
home. The moon was full. He noticed a figure
following him. He quickened his pace, the figure
did the same. He ran, the figure ran. Turning the
corner he realised it was a dead end.
The figure stabbed him. Dead End.

Sophie Edwards
Whitcliffe Mount School, Cleckheaton

229

My Dog Died

I was shocked. I stepped outside to see what was
left of my dead, lonesome dog. I sobbed into my
hands. I missed him already. I cried and I cried and
I cried even more.
I had lost my best, greatest ever friend in the
whole world!

Jake Johnson (14)
Whitcliffe Mount School, Cleckheaton

Haunted!

The crooked old door slowly crept open, whining loudly in the quiet desolate glow of the sun, stretching through the cracks in the worn-out fence. The house was dusty and untouched like it had been empty for years. Well, that's what I thought anyway.
I soon found out it wasn't …

Amy McAllister
Whitcliffe Mount School, Cleckheaton

Untitled

A beam of first light strikes her crusty lids.
Awaking slightly, she mutters constantly under
her breath regarding someone opening the blinds,
candle-lit memories of velvety soft curtains and
her dream home still circling her thoughts.
Her boyfriend has given her the perfect breakfast,
she can't believe it. *Wow!*

Raad Gorji
Whitcliffe Mount School, Cleckheaton

The Man In the Car

I could hear the rustling of the trees. Just then a
car pulled up at the side of me! A man stepped
out. I thought it was my dad but he was holding a
gun!
Startled, I started running towards the village.
I heard footsteps getting louder! He was coming!

Holly Beech-Clough
Whitcliffe Mount School, Cleckheaton

233

Tracked

They were tracking him and he didn't know how far they were. The snow crunched unwelcomingly under his boot. Wolves would never move this slowly under these conditions. A fleeting shadow passed by his feet. The last thing he saw was a great wolf in front of him. Then nothing.

Thomas McVey

Whitcliffe Mount School, Cleckheaton

Behind The Door

Bang! I was woken by a sudden noise. I scuttled to
my feet, making as little sound as possible, apart
from my now heavy breathing. I crept along the
landing and reached the room from which the
banging came. I opened the door …
'Boo!'

Stephanie Kiss

Whitcliffe Mount School, Cleckheaton

The Other Side

Robin crossed the road without taking her eyes off the shimmers, twinkling from behind the trees leading to the Reserve's woods. Close now, it seemed like a silver blanket reflecting back her surroundings. She reached forward to touch it but instead of feeling the strange anomaly, her hand just disappeared.

Tayler Wells

Whitcliffe Mount School, Cleckheaton

Horror

When Sam walked in, it was dark. He flicked on the light and walked into the kitchen. There, with a knife through her stomach, was his wife. Huddled in the corner was the black shape of a man.
The figure rose, took a step forward and said, 'You're next!'

Matthew Clough (13)
Whitcliffe Mount School, Cleckheaton

Daylight

Alone in the dark, not an ideal place to be when zombies are around every corner … No matter, I have to get to the roof, to daylight. I slowly edge around a corner; gazing down the bloodstained corridor, I only see a dead body lying under a flickering light.

Danny Barker
Whitcliffe Mount School, Cleckheaton

Joe And His Money Problems

Joe had a moment of inspiration. *Sell my brother,* he thought, *but my mum will be really upset.* He thought again, *murder my parents and take all of their money! Erm ... no, let's not.* He thought again. *What about my sister?* He thought again and again. *What can I do?*

Luke Johnson (14)

Whitcliffe Mount School, Cleckheaton

239

The Haunted House

Running through the haunted house, you could hear a scream. I'm sorry to say that was me. Downstairs there was a ghost. It was green, the ghost looked angry. It chased me. I was on the top floor, the only way down was back the way I'd come.
Trapped!

Lewis Goodyer (14)
Whitcliffe Mount School, Cleckheaton

One Too Many

Whilst I was in the south of France, I went to see
a live singer. He was pretty good. When I was
there I had a shandy.
Anyway, back to the story. I was about to leave,
saying goodbye to the singer, when I banged my
head. *'Ouch!'*

William Hardy
Whitcliffe Mount School, Cleckheaton

Untitled

Playing in the creepy, abandoned house, was
Jimmy. He was with his friends, messing about.
They all heard a noise from upstairs. Suddenly this
ugly, mysterious thing ran downstairs screaming,
so the lads sprinted, scared and exhilarated, all
the way back home.

Conner Luke Phillips

Whitcliffe Mount School, Cleckheaton

A Fishy Tale

Fishing with my mate, caught a couple of fish but not much. Suddenly my mate's rod went, he got dragged around the lake by a carp. The line gave way on the second time round. Swimming to the side of the water, he got out and laughed!
So did I!

John Britton (14)

Whitcliffe Mount School, Cleckheaton

243

Midnight

That night, me and some friends went to town.
We were really excited till we started hearing
footsteps behind us. We all looked at each other
with scared faces. We didn't know what to do.
The footsteps started getting louder.
I turned around to see a dark figure, then …

Xavia Timothy
Whitcliffe Mount School, Cleckheaton

Old Forest

It was a dark, gloomy night when Jenny took her dog, Spot, for a walk through the old forest. She jumped as she stepped on the crackling autumn leaves. They saw a light in the distance so they tiptoed towards it. She moved a branch from her face to see …

Georgia Grogan
Whitcliffe Mount School, Cleckheaton

What's Out There?

It was late at night, the sky was clear and there was a full moon. Sophie and Daisy were huddled together in a tent, telling ghost stories. Suddenly something landed on top of the tent which shook it violently. The girls screamed in horror. What was it? Who was there?

Amie Garfield (13)

Whitcliffe Mount School, Cleckheaton

Horse Days

I was riding my horse to my friend's house and we went riding in my field. We started cantering and Bobby did an immediate stop. He chucked me off and I landed on the grass, not being able to breathe, whilst Bobby was standing looking at me with puppy eyes.

Paige Ives

Whitcliffe Mount School, Cleckheaton

Doze To Remember

I got off my bus about a week ago. I was going home and when I was getting my bag and my belongings, the bus stopped. When I got off, I smacked my head hard on the wing mirror … Now I have just woken up! Where am I now?

Ashley Davies
Whitcliffe Mount School, Cleckheaton

Toilet Roll

I was at a restaurant with my friend and she asked me to go to the toilet with her, so I did.
When we were coming back I noticed she had a long line of toilet roll stuck to the bottom of her shoe.
What a red face!

Lauren Clark (13)

Whitcliffe Mount School, Cleckheaton

Holiday Showdown

I was walking towards the sea when my dad
startled me. Our key for our apartment had gone
missing. I went into the sea to look for it.
'Ouch!' A jellyfish stung me. I ran to my mum. She
took me to a café to put vinegar on it.

William Deakin

Whitcliffe Mount School, Cleckheaton

Incy Wincy

I was four years old and Mum put me to bed. I
saw something on the wall, it had eight legs and
its shadow was huge! I daren't move, just in case
it got me. I was too scared to run to the light.
Anyway, it was only a spider.

Ross Anthony Clough
Whitcliffe Mount School, Cleckheaton

251

Over The Top

It was early morning. The morning that was sure
to be our last. I could smell the fear around me in
the front line trench. We all knew we were going
over. The time passed so slowly. The whistle
went.
I jumped over, 'My head!' My war was over!

James Hendry
Whitcliffe Mount School, Cleckheaton

The Wicked Stepmother!

The orphans lived with their stepmother, an evil
woman, who worked the siblings from dawn
till dusk.
The eldest and cleverest of the children formed
a plan; they would trick the tyrant into a room,
while they ran away never to be seen again,
and that's what they did.

Ben McDonald (14)
Whitcliffe Mount School, Cleckheaton

We Love You

The door creaked open, I bellowed, 'Mum, Dad.'
I searched the house and couldn't find anyone. All
I could hear were the creaking floorboards. Fear
passed right through me. I went to the cellar …
Mum and Dad, just hanging from the roof, a little
note beside them, 'We love you!'

Cameron Bell (14)

Whitcliffe Mount School, Cleckheaton

War

Sleeping in the trenches, fighting on no-man's-land.
Shooting at my enemy, seems fine I guess. Clothes
covered in blood. Dead corpses lying in trenches
and no-man's-land. But now, as my best friend lies
dead from battle, I understand what's happening.
It's just plain killing. I'm right!

Georgie Holmes
Whitcliffe Mount School, Cleckheaton

Size Matters Not

Small and wimpy is never a good look in school.
Big and beefy always wins.
Head down, avoiding attention, small and wimpy
anxiously waits for the bus. Big and beefy lumbers
close growling, 'Money. *Now!*'
Small and wimpy grins. Only he knows who the
Yorkshire kick-boxing champion is … Him!

Alex Clayton (13)
Whitcliffe Mount School, Cleckheaton

Fear

I can hear him getting closer, branches breaking,
bushes shaking. I'm running as fast as I can to get
away, what is it? My heart's pounding, my breath
short. I've got to get away. I fall, I panic, it's black,
I'm pounced upon. '*Argh!* It's my dog, what a
relief!'

Bradley Kirk
Whitcliffe Mount School, Cleckheaton

This Is My Song

I'm in a bar. The light is dim. The air is thick with smoke and alcohol. I walk to the stage and climb the small step, then sling the guitar strap around my neck. The microphone is switched on ready for my introduction, 'Hello, I'm Saul, this is my song.'

Saul Sceats (14)

Whitcliffe Mount School, Cleckheaton

Untitled

One night I was walking home on my own from
my friend's house. I was really scared. No sound.
It was as quiet as a mouse. I could see my shadow
on the floor as I walked past a street light.
Suddenly a car pulled up and dragged me in.

Leah Smith

Whitcliffe Mount School, Cleckheaton

The Chinese Man In Bush

With bullets flying everywhere, Liam Mort had to think fast. Trying not to get shot, running through the Vietnamese forest, Liam and his troops were killing everyone in their path. Then, just out of nowhere, a crazy Chinese man came screaming out of a bush and stabbed Liam.

Thomas Richardson

Whitcliffe Mount School, Cleckheaton

The Wheelbarrow

They were celebrating in a wheelbarrow, then it
zoomed down the hill and shot out of sight and
people were screaming. Although they couldn't
stop the fast speed was keeping it balanced. Then
they hit a store and a Russian guy came over and
said, 'Are you OK everyone?'

Jake Lambert (13)

Whitcliffe Mount School, Cleckheaton

Screwed

Alone in the dark, I've just hit the wall. Lights start
shining on me with hands smothering my face
and body, brutally dragging me to the ground. I
struggle to break free, fail!
I wake up in a small, tight cell, with blood
everywhere. Then I realise that I'm screwed!

Jake Inman
Whitcliffe Mount School, Cleckheaton

Hunted

I sprinted towards my house at full pace. I barged my way through the solid wooden doors. Then I pushed my way into the front room, screaming at my wife, 'He's found us!' She dashed towards me. As I turned around, I felt the impact of the bullet pound me.

Robert Davey (13)

Whitcliffe Mount School, Cleckheaton

Adrenaline

I ran through the alley. It was dark. The alleyway
was coughing smoke and spluttering dust in my
face. I ran as fast as I could, as fast as my legs
would go. Yet somehow, something was pulling
me back. Wait! This was not paranormal -
it was a man!
Help!

Cameron Robson (14)

Whitcliffe Mount School, Cleckheaton

Bad Dream!

One day a boy went for a walk through the
woods. He got lost and didn't know where to go.
He kept on heading left, thinking he would end up
at a house, but he didn't!
'Brad,' shouted his mum.
Phew! he thought, *it was only a dream!*

Michael Craig (13)
Whitcliffe Mount School, Cleckheaton

Lost

It was very dark and I needed to get home, as my mother would be worried sick. It was getting darker and darker by the second, so I started to run. Running to a place that I didn't know. Just running aimlessly until I tripped, and then I saw it …

Oliver Hunt

Whitcliffe Mount School, Cleckheaton

The Abandoned House

One day Laura and I went to the abandoned
house. We walked down the drive slowly, turned
the creaky door handle, pushed the door open
and walked in. We dared each other to enter
rooms. The final room looked empty, but hidden
in the corner was a chair that rocked …

Emma Rhodes

Whitcliffe Mount School, Cleckheaton

The Strange House

Amie opened the big wooden doors with shiny gold handles. Amie walked over the creaky floorboards and made her way into the garden. She walked down the cobbly path towards the pond.
All of a sudden a big crash sounded behind her. What was that big, fluffy, white thing?

Emma Stirk

Whitcliffe Mount School, Cleckheaton

Creature

It was a dark night and Sarah was walking home through the forest. She heard some loud screeching. *I wonder what that is?* she thought, as she went to investigate.
When she reached the middle of the forest, the screeches got louder and louder. Then suddenly, it all went black …

Louise Reynolds
Whitcliffe Mount School, Cleckheaton

The Hazardous Forest

Tina walked through the hazardous forest.
Every step she took, she could hear crunching
leaves beneath her feet. She heard the sound of
something running after her, so she started to
run. She could see a figure behind her. She turned
around. The growling figure pounced
on top of her …

Jade Louise Mair
Whitcliffe Mount School, Cleckheaton

End Of The World

There was blood everywhere and endless bodies
on the floor. The world seemed to have ended
and everyone had gone.
Then my Xbox crashed.

Nathan Oakey
Whitcliffe Mount School, Cleckheaton

The Delicous-Tasting Chicken Slasher!

The evil man brought down the knife and slashed
the chicken in half. I grimaced as I saw it …
He then sold it to me for £5.99 which was a
reasonable price, if I do say so myself.
That night I sat down and ate it for my tea.
Delicious!

Bradley Marsden
Whitcliffe Mount School, Cleckheaton

'Argh!'

I limped away from the terrifying zombie, but it managed to anchor its ghostly hand into my blood-infested ankle. I endured a huge sear of pain. I tried to bat it off with my other leg, but the pain overcame me!
'Wake up!' Oh … it was just a dream!

Joe Bradley
Whitcliffe Mount School, Cleckheaton

Waiting

I am waiting in the queue to go on the world's fastest ride. Only two minutes to go. One part of me is urging to go on, the other is scared. Damn, it's my turn! I step into the cart. I'm at the top. I'm going down! Phew, it's over!

Jack Daniels

Whitcliffe Mount School, Cleckheaton

Mini Marvels Yorkshire & Lincolnshire

Information

We hope you have enjoyed reading this book - and that you will continue to enjoy it in the coming years.

If you like reading and writing, drop us a line or give us a call and we'll send you a free information pack. Alternatively visit our website at
www.youngwriters.co.uk

Write to:

Young Writers Information,
Remus House,
Coltsfoot Drive,
Peterborough,
PE2 9JX

Tel: (01733) 890066
Email: youngwriters@forwardpress.co.uk